With
One Foot
in the
Butterfly
Farm

Books by Louis Daniel Brodsky

Poetry

Five Facets of Myself   (1967)* (1995)

The Easy Philosopher   (1967)* (1995)

"A Hard Coming of It" and Other Poems   (1967)* (1995)

The Foul Rag-and-Bone Shop   (1967)* (1969, exp.)* (1995, exp.)

Points in Time   (1971)* (1995) (1996)

Taking the Back Road Home   (1972)* (1997) (2000)

Trip to Tipton and Other Compulsions   (1973)* (1997)

"The Talking Machine" and Other Poems   (1974)* (1997)

Tiffany Shade   (1974)* (1997)

Trilogy: A Birth Cycle   (1974) (1998)

Cold Companionable Streams   (1975)* (1999)

Monday's Child   (1975) (1998)

Preparing for Incarnations   (1975)* (1976, exp.) (1999) (1999, exp.)

The Kingdom of Gewgaw   (1976) (2000)

Point of Americas II   (1976) (1998)

La Preciosa   (1977) (2001)

Stranded in the Land of Transients   (1978) (2000)

The Uncelebrated Ceremony of Pants-Factory Fatso   (1978) (2001)

Birds in Passage   (1980) (2001)

Résumé of a Scrapegoat   (1980) (2001)

Mississippi Vistas: Volume One of *A Mississippi Trilogy*   (1983) (1990)

You Can't Go Back, Exactly   (1988, two eds.) (1989) (2003, exp.)

The Thorough Earth   (1989)

Four and Twenty Blackbirds Soaring   (1989)

Falling from Heaven: Holocaust Poems of a Jew and a Gentile
   (with William Heyen)   (1991)

Forever, for Now: Poems for a Later Love   (1991)

Mistress Mississippi: Volume Three of *A Mississippi Trilogy*   (1992)

A Gleam in the Eye: Volume One of *The Seasons of Youth*   (1992) (2009)

Gestapo Crows: Holocaust Poems   (1992)

The Capital Café: Poems of Redneck, U.S.A.   (1993)

Disappearing in Mississippi Latitudes: Volume Two of *A Mississippi Trilogy*   (1994)

A Mississippi Trilogy: A Poetic Saga of the South   (1995)*

Paper-Whites for Lady Jane: Poems of a Midlife Love Affair   (1995)

The Complete Poems of Louis Daniel Brodsky: Volume One, 1963–1967
   (edited by Sheri L. Vandermolen)   (1996)

Three Early Books of Poems by Louis Daniel Brodsky, 1967–1969: *The Easy Philosopher*,
   "A Hard Coming of It" and Other Poems, and *The Foul Rag-and-Bone Shop*
   (edited by Sheri L. Vandermolen)   (1997)

The Eleventh Lost Tribe: Poems of the Holocaust   (1998)

Toward the Torah, Soaring: Poems of the Renascence of Faith   (1998)

Voice Within the Void: Poems of *Homo supinus*   (2000)

Rabbi Auschwitz: Poems of the Shoah   (2000)*

The Swastika Clock: Endlösung Poems   (2001)*

Shadow War: A Poetic Chronicle of September 11 and Beyond, Volume One   (2001) (2004)

The Complete Poems of Louis Daniel Brodsky: Volume Two, 1967–1976
    (edited by Sheri L. Vandermolen)   (2002)

Shadow War: A Poetic Chronicle of September 11 and Beyond, Volume Two   (2002) (2004)

Shadow War: A Poetic Chronicle of September 11 and Beyond, Volume Three   (2002) (2004)

Shadow War: A Poetic Chronicle of September 11 and Beyond, Volume Four   (2002) (2004)

Shadow War: A Poetic Chronicle of September 11 and Beyond, Volume Five   (2002) (2004)

Heavenward   (2003)*

Regime Change: Poems of America's Showdown with Iraq, Volume One   (2003)*

Regime Change: Poems of America's Showdown with Iraq, Volume Two   (2003)*

Regime Change: Poems of America's Showdown with Iraq, Volume Three   (2003)*

The Complete Poems of Louis Daniel Brodsky: Volume Three, 1976–1980
    (edited by Sheri L. Vandermolen)   (2004)

Peddler on the Road: Days in the Life of Willy Sypher   (2005)

Combing Florida's Shores: Poems of Two Lifetimes   (2006)

Showdown with a Cactus: Poems Chronicling the Prickly Struggle Between the Forces
    of Dubya-ness and Enlightenment, 2003–2006   (2006)

A Transcendental Almanac: Poems of Nature   (2006)

Once upon a Small-Town Time: Poems of America's Heartland   (2007)

Still Wandering in the Wilderness: Poems of the Jewish Diaspora   (2007)

The Location of the Unknown: Shoah Poems   (2008)*

The World Waiting to Be: Poems About the Creative Process   (2008)

The Complete Poems of Louis Daniel Brodsky: Volume Four, 1981–1985
    (edited by Sheri L. Vandermolen)   (2008)

Dine-Rite: Breakfast Poems   (2008)

Kampf: Poems of the Holocaust   (2009)*

Bibliography *(coedited with Robert Hamblin)*

Selections from the William Faulkner Collection of Louis Daniel Brodsky:
    A Descriptive Catalogue   (1979)

Faulkner: A Comprehensive Guide to the Brodsky Collection: Volume I: The Biobibliography   (1982)

Faulkner: A Comprehensive Guide to the Brodsky Collection: Volume II: The Letters   (1984)

Faulkner: A Comprehensive Guide to the Brodsky Collection: Volume III: *The De Gaulle Story*   (1984)

Faulkner: A Comprehensive Guide to the Brodsky Collection: Volume IV: *Battle Cry*   (1985)

Faulkner: A Comprehensive Guide to the Brodsky Collection: Volume V: Manuscripts and
    Documents   (1989)

Country Lawyer and Other Stories for the Screen by William Faulkner   (1987)

Stallion Road: A Screenplay by William Faulkner   (1989)

Biography

William Faulkner, Life Glimpses   (1990)

Fiction

Between Grief and Nothing *(novel)*   (1964)*

Between the Heron and the Wren *(novel)*   (1965)*

"Dink Phlager's Alligator" and Other Stories   (1966)*

The Drift of Things *(novel)*   (1966)*

Vineyard's Toys *(novel)*   (1967)*

The Bindle Stiffs *(novel)*   (1968)*

Yellow Bricks *(short fictions)*   (1999)

Catchin' the Drift o' the Draft *(short fictions)*   (1999)

This Here's a Merica *(short fictions)*   (1999)

Leaky Tubs *(short fictions)*   (2001)

Rated Xmas *(short fictions)*   (2003)

Nuts to You! *(short fictions)*   (2004)

Pigskinizations *(short fictions)*   (2005)

With One Foot in the Butterfly Farm *(short fictions)*   (2009)

Memoir

The Adventures of the Night Riders, Better Known as the Terrible Trio
   (with Richard Milsten)   (1961)*

* *Unpublished*

With One Foot in the Butterfly Farm

Short fictions

by L.D. Brodsky

TIME BEING BOOK**S**
POETRY IN SIGHT AND SOUND

An imprint of Time Being Press
St. Louis, Missouri

Time Being Books®
10411 Clayton Road
St. Louis, Missouri 63131

Time Being Books® is an imprint of Time Being Press®, St. Louis, Missouri.
Time Being Press® is a 501(c)(3) not-for-profit corporation.
Time Being Books® volumes are printed on acid-free paper.

The characters and events portrayed in these stories are fictitious. Any similarities to real persons, living or dead, are purely coincidental and not intended by the author.

ISBN 978-1-56809-129-7 (Paperback)

Library of Congress Cataloging-in-Publication Data:

Brodsky, Louis Daniel.
    With one foot in the butterfly farm : short fictions / by L.D. Brodsky.—
1st ed.
        p. cm.
    ISBN 978-1-56809-129-7 (pbk. : alk. paper)
    I. Title.
    PS3552.R623W57 2009
    813'.54—dc22
                                                                        2009031857

Cover design by Jeff Hirsch
Cover photo copyrighted by and reprinted with permission of Jeff Hirsch
Book design and typesetting by Trilogy M. Mattson

Manufactured in the United States of America

First Edition, first printing (2009)

Acknowledgments

Once again, I must express gratitude to my two devoted editors at Time Being Books, Sheri Vandermolen and Jerry Call. The clarity and the sparkle of these stories exist, in no small measure, because of their persistence and patience with me. I thank them both for their dedication to the cause.

Contents

With One Foot in the Butterfly Farm

Apt. 18 B–D
Going Down

Though you'd descended, times beyond record, from your eighteenth-story apartment to the lobby or basement parking garage, you couldn't recall ever having heard her voice, those beguiling female articulations emanating from somewhere in the elevator, which abruptly arrived at your floor, opened its doors, and beckoned you to enter.

"Going down."

Curiously, her two words struck you as ominous.

Were you losing your gourd? Had she always been riding the elevator, with you? Who was she? Of what origin? What did she look like?

The doors shut, like the lids of a giant clamshell.

"Going down," she repeated. You held your breath, hoping the car wasn't the *Titanic*.

Then, you were in a limbo of controlled free fall, that hiatus when your hands grip the rails, your ears listen for aberrant sounds, and you pray that, having placed yourself in fate's hands, you'll once again be spared a lethal plunge — a squashing of your guts, in a trash compactor.

"Lobby. Going up."

Safe! Safe again! You stepped out, onto the maze of green runner, into the forsythia-yellow halls, and headed for the mailboxes.

But before you could open 18 B–D's, with your Schlage key, the excruciatingly obese building manager, Edie, spilled over into your space, caught you up short, eager to engage you, in conversation. You winced.

"Sorry to bother you, Mr. Intravenous, but would you mind if I ask you something?"

Before you could say yes, she barged ahead.

"I'm taking a poll of the residents as to what everyone thinks about the voice."

"The *what?*" you mumbled, genuinely perplexed.

"The new lady we installed in all three elevators."

"Oh, her . . . she . . . them . . . whoever. She's sexy."

"Excuse me? That's *my* voice, a recording."

You bit your tongue, wondering what to say next, how to conceal your blush (you'd turned second-degree red). Edie Sphinx flushed.

"Mr. Intravenous! *Really!*"

For the next three weeks, you trudged up and down the eighteen flights of stairs.

But every day, on returning home from work, exiting the fire-escape well, you found a fresh rose, in a bud vase, by your door.

Tree of Life

There once was a young man who grew old overnight, in the single spell of a November night's sleep, older than a sequoia or bristlecone pine, so old, in reality, that he awakened behind Moses' eyes and believed, in all good faith, with all his might, that he was of Biblical times reborn, a sage in the likeness of Abraham, Isaac, and Jacob.

But for all the spiritual inspiration this miracle delivered to the young man, who, overnight, grew into a tree, assumed the likeness of Old Testament patriarchs, one unwanted side effect appeared to him, in his bathroom mirror, refused to accord him respect, horrified him, such was the nature of his transmutation: his skin had turned into inch-thick bark.

Arrested in stupefaction, utter fear, he stared at his bare physique, wrapped in ghastly, wizened disfigurement, wondering what he might do to remove this curse, at least how to disguise himself, for now, hide from the curious, the freak-seekers, the greedy media, society at large, his immediate circle of friends, and backstabbers at the office, who coveted his position.

But try as he might, applying astringents and emollients (witch hazel, Vaseline with aloe, K-Y Jelly), spraying himself with bottles of Chaps, Brut, Lilac Vegetal, resorting to cleaning products under his kitchen sink (Endust, Windex, Tilex, Clorox, Formula 409), he couldn't debark his body or even get his business suit over it.

In a fit of frantic insanity, he began ripping thousands of needles off his limbs.

Dinosaurs

Admittedly, for the past forty-five years, I've prided myself on my inordinately outsize lexicon, my polysyllabic vocabulary, my plethoric verbal armada, my labyrinthine ganglion of stentorianly imperious words that would cause that curmudgeonly hubristic Dr. Johnson to go paroxysmal in his pedantic tracks, query, flummoxedly, why he'd even try to compile the most comprehensive dictionary ever assembled, for the capacious English language, cognizant that my word-hoard relegates his to shame's quagmire.

It's no phenomenological surprise, then, this prandial hour, as I repose here, in my neighborhood café, preparing to versify, that chef Joe, aware I'm a poet of intergalactic renown, imminently deserving of the myriad praiseworthy accolades I've garnered for my gargantuan repository of mother-tongue signifiers, would request that I deign to compete with his staff, which has made three score and fifteen words out of "dinosaurs."

Cornucopiously flattered that Joe's culinary entourage has thrown down its collective gauntlet, I know, incontrovertibly, that, having been published in *Harper's*, I have no recourse but to parry and thrust my épée at the college-aged junta of amateur lingual prestidigitators.

(And there's an additional incentive for my opening my notebook and writing, atop a pristine leaf, where I'd scribe a poem title, "dinosaurs": complimentary repast, when I prevail.)

But after fidgeting in my booth, for nigh onto an hour, cogitating, tergiversating, ratiocinating, cerebrating, lucubrating, nay perspiring more ragingly than my condensating water tumbler, over the appellation affixed to those primordial reptilian beasts, I begin to grow decidedly alabastrine, then porphyritic, then apoplectic, seeing that all I have to show for my travail are "a," "I," "or," "so," "no," "in," "on," and "do."

Chef Joe inquires, from the kitchen, "How ya doin'?"

As Laura delivers my provender, I brush past her, toward the egress.

Now, it's 12:49 a.m. I'm restively writhing, moistening my sheets, counting, reiteratively, my octet of words — dinosaurian sheep — hoping they'll lull me to sleep, not stomp and eat me.

The Magical Seeds

One day long, long ago, almost longer than forgetting can even begin to remember, you lost your way while going to Salacious Faire, that fabled iniquitous purlieus where rambunctious young country boys and girls went to play rough-and-tumble games of love.

You left home, with exceedingly high hopes, never imagining that you'd not return to your parents, your siblings, your pet pig, Squiggles, buoyed by dreams of converting your magical seeds into something altogether sensational, something akin to wonder, dazzlement, rapture.

But such was not to be your destiny, not that day, anyway, when you headed off, under heady steam, for Salacious Faire. Indeed, you weren't more than hours into the journey, when highwaymen accosted you, forced you to surrender your amazing seeds.

By the time you arrived, three days later, at Salacious Faire, it had disbanded. The grounds were desolate — no tents, pennons, stalls, no dizzying busyness, just matted grass, animal puckey, wagon-wheel ruts, in a vast, empty field in the middle of nowhere. You were disoriented, destitute, despondent, scared.

Then it was, having no place to go, that a lady of questionable origin, disreputable intent, possessing a more-than-checkered past, invited you home, to her hovel, under Lewd Bridge. Having no competing options, you agreed to be seduced; after all, she could keep the rain off your head.

Days turned into years, in a flash of passing distractions. The two of you gave birth to twin urchins. Often, you told her of your stolen magical seeds. Always, she listened, with a sympathetic ear, albeit not comprehending their astonishing potential. She compassionately endured your "if only" mantra.

One day, maybe twenty-five years later, it suddenly dawned on you that your traumatic loss had, unwittingly, been your gain, that the seeds you'd not arrived with, at Salacious Faire, had, in reality, played their magical part in connecting you with your unimagined life.

The Revolt of the Clothes

It started, not altogether innocuously, with his attaché case's taking leave of its senses, heading off to work, independent of him.

After a month of that peculiarly inexplicable behavior, his black wing tips and argyles followed suit (two weeks earlier, his three-piece business-stripe suit had driven to Micro-Acme, accompanied only by his tie and starched white shirt), kicked back at his office, putting themselves up on his desk.

And if that wasn't perplexing and frustrating enough — losing control over his wardrobe — even his toupee began making the trek, on its own.

After ten weeks of that monkey business, his boss was at a loss for thoughts, words, as was he. His clothes were wearing him out.

When his three-day-soiled-and-stained underpants got up the gumption to leave home and ended up in his cubicle, airing all his discontents with company policy, sabotaging the quarterly reports, he phoned his section leader, to plead innocence.

By that time, in his conspicuous absence (presence?), he'd become the butt of the scandalous scuttlebutt infesting and infecting corporate headquarters. His reputation, thanks to his prodigal clothes, had reached a low so degrading, he was cashiered.

Worse than that were his future prospects. For a year, his wardrobe sent out résumés, but who would hire just wing tips and argyles or a three-piece suit or filthy underpants or a toupee?

High-School Buddies

You had a prolonged lunch, recently, at an old hangout, with three buddies from your high-school days, guys you've seen every so often, over the past half-century since graduation, once — and sort of still — friends for life, who'd all vowed never to lose touch yet succumbed to time's remorseless cancellations of your Tom-and-Huck blood pact meant to seal youth's rites-of-passage bonds.

After dismissing, in decidedly short order, the results of the recent election, fearing you'd offend each other's political sensibilities, and exhausting the minimal residue of small talk, centering on wives, grandkids, retirement, pastimes, you advanced to the one topic of common concern: the status of your physical conditions.

Suddenly, the conversation grew animated, which was a godsend that really brought you together.

One of you was recovering from prostate-cancer surgery; another, your resident all-conference halfback, was sporting two new, titanium-alloy-and-polyethylene knees; a third was breathing thanks to a porcine mitral valve; and you, who'd been pissing blood, over Christmas, had just been diagnosed with bladder stones.

You spared them no details about the procedure — catheter, penis pain, photos of your innards, the plan to send a crushing tool (a lithotrite) up your tool, to save the day, a day of infamy (tantamount to December 7, 1941), the following week, which you were praying would fall off the calendar.

And so it went, your once-in-a-blue-moon get-together, for very old time's sake.

Later that otherwise wholly uninspired afternoon, after you'd had a chance to meditate on the degradation of your physiologically challenged buddies, you weren't altogether certain how to feel.

Who needs old friends, you questioned, surmised, *if they remind you of time's raping, pillaging, plundering? Without them, I just might forget to die.*

Apt. 6 A
Prize Art Nouveau Bedroom Suite

Though it had been seven years or more since he discovered and bought his prize bedroom suite, at the Golden Oldies Antique Mall, he could still recall the pockmarked dealer, who'd delivered and assembled the bed frame and armoire, installed the tall wall mirror, nightstand, vanity, and told him that the set had been stored in his barn — thus the reason some pieces showed worm damage.

"But not to worry. There's nothin' active. Trust me." Which he did.

The set was gorgeous — high Art Nouveau, French, some sort of fruitwood, textured with variegated veneers, each piece decorated, extensively, with dazzling glued-on iris-tendril whiplashes, giving it the appearance of frenetic movement.

That the full-size bed squeaked chronically was perfectly understandable. After all, it hadn't been constructed, a century earlier, to accommodate a tall, obese American, rather two diminutive French people doubtless weighing far less, together, than he.

But for three years, off and on, he'd been hearing the eight-foot-tall armoire, with its oversize beveled mirror covering the door, creak and groan like a tree in a windstorm. This he did find strange, curious, disconcerting. It was as if it were trying to communicate with him. Indeed, it almost seemed to be grumbling, complaining, begging him to take notice.

Yesterday morning, when he pushed on it, it collapsed, broke apart, with a thunderous, cascading crash, disrupting his orderly bedroom, the enormous door's glass shattering helter-skelter.

Terrified, he called the high-rise's maintenance engineer, who promised he'd have the shambles removed by the time he returned home, from work. That evening, the space created by the missing armoire became a black hole, into which his dreams strayed and got lost.

Sometime after midnight, he was startled awake by a swarming of painfully biting sensations steadily gnawing away at his sweaty flesh.

Thelma

Normally, I try like Jehoshaphat to forget how many times my wife's nagged me into changing my last will and testament, each time kvetching me into ceding another chunk of my retirement's Pangaea to her greedy desire to end up with all of me when Mr. Oblivion finally opens his door and invites me to sit shiva for my destitute soul. But seeing "Eighteenth Edition" on my will brings it right home.

Jesus! I don't mind saying what a bitch she's been — Thelma, my third wife. And now, my own kids, by Zelda, are left penniless. It's the awful price I've had to pay, the last ten years, to keep Thelma a slave to all my physical needs — feeding, showering, dressing, pissing and shitting me.

Making all these legal changes hasn't exactly been cheap, either, I can tell you. Lawyers are shysters, goniffs, Shylocks; mine's the worst.

But on our most recent taxi ride over to his office, a brainstorm came to me, and I had Shakestein incorporate it into my will.

He opined that my cemetery (it's as Orthodox as a three-dollar bill, usually, allowing every Saul, Abe, and Moishe in, for the right shekels) just might not look favorably, in fact frown, on executing my instructions from the other side.

"Write it up, my legal-eagle beagle," I cajoled Shakestein.

Thelma grew faint, fanned herself, with his business card, when I ordered Mr. $500-an-Hour-Pettifogger to perform his shell game for his paying customer — me.

"What I want to include in my nineteenth will is this: one gravestone for the two of us — me and Thelma. Above my name, 'Fuck 'Em'; under hers, 'And Her, Too.'"

The Loading Dock

One completely unpremeditated day (an early afternoon in late May, to be precise), you walked away from work, out of your own life, and never looked over your shoulder or bothered to return, rather kept going, toward a location for which your imagination could hardly have prepared you: the hole in your broken soul, through which all your emotions, dreams, élan vital had, like ozone, previously leaked, leaving your spirit gasping for reasons to endure, continue breathing, being — a hole through which your body, too, would soon sublime.

How long you were gone was a matter of conjecture to absolutely no one in the stratospheric altitudes that buoyed your disappearance. The only thing that mattered was that you'd relegated your future to the past, without having to come to terms with your termination.

By sheer volition, you'd exempted yourself from having to acquiesce to death, navigate the hazards and rigors of its inflexible attitude . . . or so you'd assumed, in your otherworldly solitude, until one completely unpremeditated day (an early afternoon in late May, to be precise), when you walked back into work, from your ten-minute break, back into your life of silent desperation, safe, nonetheless, in your consoling corpo-reality, for during that brief Lucky Strike recess, standing out there, alone, on the loading dock, you'd sensed the strangest premonition come over you, almost as though some inimical force within the cigarette were compelling you to surrender to its smoke, follow it, through a hole in your broken soul.

Wal-Mart

Perhaps it was a fierce sense of loyalty, civic pride, that, until today, kept him shopping the square. He'd always preferred patronizing the main-street merchants.

As he passed the gargantuan parking lot at the city limits, in view of the interstate, something drew him into the shopping center's vortex. Locating a space in front of the brand-new Wal-Mart Superstore, he entered the nearest door — the eye of an elephant — and was sucked into a maelstrom of commerce.

The sheer crush, press, pell-mell mill of people was dizzying. He was a leaky tub on a tempestuous ocean, flotsam in a sea of foreign merchandise. He'd never visited such a bizarre bazaar, been imprisoned in a Marrakesh-like importer's emporium — stuff, things, items, products, doodads, gewgaws, crap.

Most every label he scrutinized displayed a country of origin other than the U.S.A. — Korea, Mexico, India, China . . . China . . . China . . . China.

For an hour, he browsed, growing confused, depressed, dour, becoming more disillusioned by the aisle. The buzz of shopper-drones in the hive grew deafening. How had he allowed himself to stray so far from the square? He knew not a soul in this suburb called Wal-Mart, though he'd lived in his small town for forty years.

His soles ached. His head was home to a migraine. He had to pee extra bad but couldn't find an "associate" to direct him to the restroom, nor could he get his bearings in the cavernous space.

Drenching his khakis, in front of the gurgling fishtanks, his whole body went cold as an iced mackerel.

Damn good thing his accident happened at Wal-Mart, and it was an even happier accident that, not four aisles away, was the men's department. Luckily, he found "Consuela G.," who was not only perky and helpful but tactful, never once mentioning, or even staring at, his urine stains. Within ten minutes, she'd outfitted him in purple warmups, replete with new neon-yellow-and-black sneakers, and gotten him through checkout.

Outside, he felt surprisingly light, young, athletic — born again. He jogged to his car, marveling at how little he'd spent. It felt really good, not having to wear a belt.

Buon appetito

How it happened (was it with "such rapidity" or "such alacrity"?) is yet, after so many days in the freezer, a matter of absolute and unadulterated conjecture.

To be sure, all you know, with any certainty, is that you bought the farm, in the flash of a jagged lightning bolt lashing its chaotic passage across a stratosphere inimical to human existence, expired as you were eating the last piece of your sixteen-inch deep-dish Sicilian pizza pie (oozing like Mount Etna, with six cheeses and all the toppings), simply slipped, slouched, undetected, to one side of your booth, that final slice, like a swollen tongue, sticking out of your mouth, an empty second bottle of cheap Valpolicella lodged between your robust gut and your crotch, like a penis boasting a Leaning Tower of Pisa erection.

Though, in a manner of speaking, you were there when the EMT's arrived at Benito Gardini's Trattoria, you were there only in body and spirits, not spirit. Your living presence was nowhere to be found.

To be as sure as sure could be, given the dire circumstances of your immediate condition, you phoned your ex-wife of twenty years, Angelica Rose, but she refused to drive to Benito's, to identify you. You couldn't reach your lawyer, Carlo Gorgonzola; even if you had, you were strapped for cash. Your two boys, Guido and Abe, were living in Alaska, with Inuits. Even if your daughter, Carmelita, had been so inclined, she couldn't have left her Orthodox husband, Yakov, with their twelve bambinos, in Jerusalem's Mea Shearim, to help put closure to your unfinished existence.

And so you passed before your very eyes, going out as you'd come in, just a kid of immigrant dagos, from Boston's North End, a fat kid, at that, grown into an even fatter numbers runner for Don Pentangeli, you a small-time exploiter of other guys' bad luck, who, at fifty-one, died with 1500 milliliters of vino and a foot-and-a-third-diameter Paisano Special, minus its eighth slice, in your cement-mixer belly . . . departed in a not-altogether-flattering quietus while dining at Gardini's Trattoria, on North Margin Street . . . who just happened to die a second time, in the Big Dig connector tunnel, when a three-ton slab of ceiling concrete collapsed, crushing the ambulance conveying you to the morgue.

To be ultimately sure, you eventually arrived there, along with the two flattened paramedics. You were unmistakably unidentifiable, as a human, save for the slice of Benito Gardini's Paisano Special pie, lodged, inextricably, between your two blue lips, which was perfectly *buon appetito* with you.

Keeper

He craves that primal, energizing thrill he gets when he flings himself from bed, with the thrusting force of an alligator's flailing tail, then gropes in his dim closet, like a hunter-gatherer, and emerges with his spoils, which he throws onto the bed, before plopping down, beside them.

The order is all important. It's become a sacred ritual, a ceremony he performs with agility and expeditiousness (after all, this tradition comes from years of practice): leopard-skin, zebra-striped, or Komodo-dragon-motif boxers; Barney the Dinosaur–print tube socks; brown-and-green-camouflage uniform; steel-toed boots.

And he's ready for work, never mind that he doesn't perform the three s's — shit, shower, and shave — until he returns home, which makes perfect sense, since he gets filthy dirty and smelly as hell, at the zoo, where he supervises a crew responsible for spraying the cages, after removing the prodigious feces of the hippos, rhinos, tapirs, and elephants, and taking care of the entire big-cat house.

He approaches his job with an eager headiness, a zest for inhaling the rank perfume of dank cement sullied with stale urine, dropped and flung dung. On his fourteen-hour shift, he's in heaven. He revels in sensing himself one with the natural world.

The animals, to an animal, welcome their keeper. They've developed a trust, almost a kinship, with him, and he has no fear that one of the beasts will charge or trample him or see him as fresh meat. They seem to appreciate their pristine habitats.

And so, with his hoses, brooms, swabs, and mops, what used to be horribly unsung days at the office (years ago, he mentored indigents, at Sunburst Ministries) are now studies in communion with the peaceable kingdom, as he serves God, one needy soul at a time.

Apt. 14 C
A Hundred and One Mantras

Nothing much was on his mind, nothing but a blind determination to die, die in the least inconvenient, most painless way, to which end he took up an intractable position, naked, in the middle of the trafficked street that rattled and screeched in front of his high-rise.

There, he assumed an attitude of serene enlightenment, with legs folded Maharishi Mahesh Yogi–like, mumbling a hundred and one unintelligible mantras, as if to invoke the agents of his demise.

And in that position, unwaveringly, uncoweringly, envisioning himself a turtle crossing I-55, he waited, waited for his inevitable annihilation to arrive, the instantaneous obliteration of his being, the numbing squash, crush, of his skeleton and guts.

But after six hours of absolutely nothing happening, nothing but the shriveling of his skin and its uncontrollable quivering, for the unabating rain, he decided to throttle his hundred and one mantras, pack it all in, call it quits, go back inside, and try again another time — take a rain check.

Though highly disappointed with the results, he embraced a stoical approach to his failed enterprise — it just wasn't his day.

Coming unfolded from his tendon-twisting asana, like a lotus opening to the warmth of the sun, he stood up and started to cross the street.

But he never reached his high-rise, because when he got to the sidewalk, he found that the building had moved to a new address.

On the Origin of Species, or The Descent of Man

Damned if I can even begin to remember just how old I might conceivably be. After all, my life span spans the life of mankind, that freakish, mysterious rise, from the primal slime, of creatures with a semblance of inchoate gray matter, a glimmer of the beginnings of a mind — a proto- or ur-human, capable of recognizing its differences from the winged, four-legged, and swimming creatures inhabiting the terraqueous planet's air, lands, and seas, herbivorous/carnivorous avians, reptiles, amphibians, fish, many far larger than my apelike likeness.

Though I can't measure my existence, in time — years, centuries, millenniums, epochs, eras — I do recall certain appellations of my protracted evolution, starting with my variations on the *Australopithecus* theme (*afarensis, africanus, robustus, boisei* . . . quite a handful of vicious, ignorant animal, there, if forgetting serves me, correctly), followed by a pugnacious trio of upright *Homos* (*habilis, erectus, sapiens neanderthalensis*) and, eventually, for the developmental *pièce de résistance*, the granddaddy of all modern humans, *Homo sapiens sapiens*, alias Cro-Magnon man.

Oh, to be sure, I've been around the block, seen my share of red-meat and vegetarian violence, known the darkest and the most highly illuminated ages, and somehow, despite planet-shuddering asteroids, the Ice Age, droughts, and atomic bombs, survived extinction, made it, intact, if considerably altered in size and intelligence, to this moment of density in four-dimensional space, when, tonight, in man's designation of circadian rhythms, I'm able to write this tribute to my origins, proclaim myself master of the universe, by virtue of having outlasted my progenitors, those haphazard ancestors of today's species of wise men, of which I'm, most assuredly, the prime exemplar.

Which leads me to ask this universe-bending question: has it really been worth all the fuss?

It Happened at
Most Precious Blood Medical Center

Open-heart surgery, in and of itself, so to speak, has proved to be the Eighth Wonder of the Modern World, an invasive catalyst for mankind's longevity, by now an almost-run-of-the-mill operation, as easy to accomplish as stanching a nosebleed.

That said, there's always the on-the-off-chance occasion, as in every near-foolproof human endeavor, that protocol won't go quite according to protocol, something will go awry, come a tumble, even among the most renowned doctors and their skilled staffs, no matter they've performed perfectly, 9,999 times.

And wouldn't you know it, you'd be the one-in-ten-thousand case, when, after your successful six-hour quintuple bypass, your severed sternum wired together, your flesh sewn shut, and after two whole days out of intensive care, they'd discover somebody had left something behind, something or any number of somethings.

Since they couldn't be certain, despite repeated MRI's and CAT scans the radiology department ran on you, it was officially decided, by Most Precious Blood's board of directors, that you needed to be opened up and emptied immediately. After all, by that time, your collapsed lungs had begun attempting to inflate fully, and the pain of some foreign object(s) retarding their expansion was nothing short of nothing else you'd ever felt. With each tentative inhalation, you'd scream bloody murder.

Suffice it to say you made the AP wire service, appeared in all the major and secondary newspapers. The story ran in sixty countries. You did eleven TV interviews, with Oprah, Lou Dobbs, Larry King, Tucker Carlson, Greta Van Susteren, Wolf Blitzer, Nancy Grace, Barbara Walters, Jay Leno, Howard Stern, and Don Imus.

Some equated your debacle with the Katrina catastrophe,

took great pains (no pun intended) to commiserate with you, as they exploited the details, by sordidly enumerating what had been salvaged from your "sunken treasure chest" — a proverbial junkyard of multifarious stuff: three hemostats; two scalpels; four inches of unused leg vein; a half-empty pack of Marlboro Lights; two champagne-bottle corks; a pair of Gucci sunglasses; three roaches and a somewhat rusted clip; a munched-on Pay-Day bar; an iPhone; a BlackBerry; a GPS bracelet, for tracking polar bears; assorted cold cuts on moldy sourdough; five plastic forks; two tickets for *The Simpsons Movie*; an illegal alien's Social Security card and passport; an Alcoholics Anonymous "One Day at a Time" medallion; an open carton of Pleasure Plus condoms; a miniature Koran, Rig-Veda, and Gideon Bible. In addition, there were myriad objects completely unidentifiable, for corruption and degradation by bodily fluids.

It appeared the team had mistaken your cavity for a trash receptacle.

To be sure, Most Precious Blood grudgingly accepted responsibility, admitted its role in the execrable debacle, copping a quick plea, agreeing to be completely cooperative, in hope of avoiding a class-action suit on behalf of all its previous open-heart patients, who, assumably, could be sporting chestfuls of "UFO's."

That you walked away from your open-and-shut-and-open case, to tell your twice-told tale of coronary woe, ranked right up there with Christ's crucifixion and resurrection.

That you lasted, as a celebrity, exactly eight days — twenty-four hours more than the one-week news cycle reserved for assassinations of presidents and popes — was a miracle.

And then the afterglow set in, faded away, to nullity. By the ninth day, you were fish wrap. Within another week, your fame had waned to anonymity itself.

Sadly, when all was said and done, you were stunned to learn that Medicare's new rule change mitigated against its paying for Most Precious Blood's "never event" and that you were in debt, to the tune of $198,000 — a sum that would render you instantaneously bankrupt, since your media earnings amounted to a paltry $22,517.

To make matters worse, for a week, you'd been experiencing chest pains again.

Two days later, you were back under the knife.

Your surgeon, Dr. Father Sergio O'Donnell, and his staff, descending into the less-than-virgin territory of your thorax, found their unaccounted-for chest retractor.

Uncle Homunculus

OK, boys, listen up. Just hold your goldarn Przewalski'ses and Clydesdales. Let's try to get one thing straight, between us, and I shore's hell don't mean what you're thinkin'. Oh, don't play coy with me, boys. I've been around the bend too many times, for a good ol' fashion leg-pullin', fell off the turnip truck enough times, in my heydays, not to recognize when I'm havin' my pud's wool pulled.

First you tell me a hungmonkulous is a deformed dwarf cooked up, in a flask, by one of them alkymists, the same guys who changed poop into fool's aluminum.

Then you try to convince me that a homo's-Uncle-Gus is a miniature unflawed speciman of a human being, hidin' in each and every male and female sperm, just waitin' to get ejacumated into a writhin' vagina or spritzed onto the floor or bedsheets, by guys chokin' their chickens, thumpin' their Thuringers.

Next, you say a hominidoculus is a tiny human being on the order of Verne Troyer and Hervé Villechaize — movie actors who made it big . . . *really* big.

And now you're tryin' to make me believe that a hum-funkulist is a human fetus, just any ol' baby that comes outta its mama's groin.

Well, boys, which is it? It can't hardly be all four of them medical theories poppyconcocted, in the fourth century B.C., by scienticians.

And while you're at it, I wish you'd cut the shit with callin' me "Uncle Homunculus." You gotta know that rubs me up and down my spine's wrong. Kinda sounds like you boys is callin' me a don't ask/don't tell, a flamer, faggot, fruit bar, fudge-packer, fairy, powder poofter, poove, queer bait, gay blade, strange plant. And in all truth, though we're longtime buds, I don't exactly take too darn kindly to your alligators, your innuendos and out the others.

And as for what a hungmonkulous really is, let me set you boys straight, between us, offer you an altogether nother interpredation of the critter: a hunk-o'-monkey-nuts is the missin' sausage link between a silverbuck lowlife gorilla and a Mongolian bonobo, an Irangutan cross-fertilized with a Piltdown man, who gave rise to the five of you bad-ass bastards, who don't know your asses from the crabgrass on Shinola's hole, your midget dorks from a dwarf's sweet-and-sour pork.

Three-Dog Nights

To be quite honest, most nights — well, every night — I prefer to dine out by myself. You might say I'm a creature of habits. I doubt I've eaten home twice in two dozen years, 'cause, in all truth, I can't stand chowing without a crowd around me. What's more, I never learned to cook, so I count on the kindness of seasoned short-order chefs, to rustle up my grub.

Most nights — every night — I prefer to dine at Café Brooklyn, in the heart of suburban St. Louis, a far cry from the Big Apple but good enough for me, 'cause "Crispy" whips up a mean quarter-pound kosher dog, which my taste buds and guts love more than most dog lovers love their Chihuahuas and corgis.

So, most nights — seven nights a week, truth be told — I order up three all-kosher-beef Hebrew National Dinner Franks (leave off the condiments, if you please), which I space out over a period of an hour and a half, while relaxing with a bottle of French Pinot Noir, to wash down those scrumptious grilled meats.

Well, as I said, I'm a fairly routine guy of habits, so I like to savor my dogs. Crispy knows just the right degree of char and sizzle.

And for sure, I consume more dogs per head, per year, than any of Café Brooklyn's other clientele (I'm definitely the most regular of all their nightly regulars).

So imagine, just the other morning, at Buffalo Bob's, where I breakfast, seven a.m.'s a week, I'm caught up short, dead to rights, by my short hairs, by the headline of an article in the local rag, about a guy named Joey Chestnut: "Man Beats World Hot Dog Eating Record." Naturally, my ears perk up, 'cause I'm such a Francophile frank freak myself (I've been a three-dog-night eater going on three decades).

I go shits over this Joey Chestnut's totally amazing feat — gobbling up 59½ HDB's (that's hot dog and buns) in a mere ten short minutes (the officially sanctioned time limit for the Fourth of July International Hot Dog Eating Contest, held, annually, at Coney Island, by Nathan's Famous), clobbering the reigning world champ's record, making Takeru Kobayashi's 53¾ dogs (last summer) seem paltry, no earth-shattering event for a major-league trencherman.

But then, Chestnut's new high-dog mark was set at the Southwest Regional Hot Dog Eating Championship, held at the Arizona Mills Mall, in Tempe, and this guy has yet to make his statement at Coney Island.

All the while, I can't help thinking that for all my years of three-dog nights, I'm just a piker. After all, do the math. This Joey Chestnut, of San Jose, just twenty-three, downed one dog every ten seconds, six per minute, while, at my optimum best (trust me), I can only park three all-kosher-beef quarter-pounder weenies every ninety minutes; that's one dog each 1800 seconds, hardly something to write home about, assuming I might be home for dinner, in the first place, since I eat out, most nights — well, every night — at the same place, where, weekly, I absorb my standard twenty-one-dog salute of Hebrew National's finest all-kosher-beef dinner franks, which, if I say so, is the record of standing at Café Brooklyn, one not likely to be surpassed, anytime soon, by anyone, save some hotshot hot-dogging hot-dog shark passing through these parts, on his way to Coney Island.

428 Degrees of Indexed Heat

Fancy-schmancy, Nancy! Hotsy-totsy! Far *out*! Nifty! Neato-Tito! Keen! Cool! Groovy! Swift! Cle-*ver*! I mean, the seasonal meteorological terminology being spewed and bally-hooed and mooed by local-TV weather jockeys.

I'm talking "heat index," "heat index," "heat index," whereby a steamy, stalled-thermal-inversion, muggy, humid 95-degree day gets miraculously escalated into a 135-Fahrenheit scorcher, just by the wave of an elaborate array of cutting-edge-technology wands, which, ultimately, work to negatively impact us all, reinforcing, facilitating, our apathetic, lethargic, sedentary lifestyles, encouraging us to stay safely indoors, air-conditioned to the nines, terrified to step outside, into our own personal Death Valleys, content to let the other guys die from overheating strokes — those who fail to heed the latest heat-index oracles.

I must confess, embarrassed though I may be, that I fit into the category of paranoid worry-wart nervous Nellies who put complete credence in TV's best and brightest weather-heads, especially whenever they prognosticate triple digits. After all, tipping the teeters at 428 pounds, I have to watch my step, steps, keep as cool as a flash-frozen cucumber, not stray too far from the oscillating fan in my basement.

I hate summers in St. Louis, like a plague of black bu-boes, hate even when I have to buy groceries (which is every other day), let alone drive, every night, over to Ted Drewes, to get my daily nutritional supplement, from three large concretes — vanilla frozen custard chock-full of Heath Bar pieces and M&M's — which help me cool off while I stand there, on the parking lot, eating that creamy-crunchy good-and-good-for-ya goodness before it melts.

Admittedly, it's a love-at-first-hate relationship I have, with St. Louis, heat indexes on TV, sweating my buns off (I wish), for a good three straight summer months, every summer, a hate-at-first-love relationship I have with my basement, dinosaurs causing greenhouse gases to escape down our exhaust pipes, pollute the stratospheres, allow the ozones to stagnate or disappear, trapping and turning the hydrogens around Earth into molten frozen custard.

And believe me, this heat doesn't make 428 pounds any easier. It makes it feel like 590, when my fat index factors in all the factors, like exercise (standing, walking — moving, in general) missed, for having to hunker down in the basement, with the oscillating fan, additional large concretes eaten, to keep cool on the parking lot, and pining like two polar bears, in heat, on separate ice floes, for wind-chill factors to freeze hell out of heat indexes.

Apt. 3 Y–Z
The Colors of Success

Awakening at 5:40, each morning, was no big deal, no federal case, just perfected routine. He could do it in his sleep, do it blindfolded, do it without the alarm. And this a.m. was no different, as his naked body rose from the depths of his sheets.

But when he crept into the bathroom, in the dark (the head was less than twenty feet from his bed), and fumbled for the light switch, it eluded him. Why, he wasn't too sure. Eventually, the halogen bulbs and the heat lamp filled the compact room with illumination.

In the twelve mirrors of varying heights and widths (every open space was covered with reflecting glass), he could see his glorious fitness-center physique. Only, his flesh was purple, as if bathed by a black light, and the toilet paper was polka-dotted blue. His turds were orange. The towels were zebra-striped. The porcelain of his toilet was smeared in Day-Glo pink. His tub and sink were fire-engine red. His copies of *Playboy* were Pantone Process Cyan.

For a few perplexed seconds, he stood transfixed, inundated by a freakish déjà vu of his roach-littered room in Haight-Ashbury; only, that was almost forty years before, back in 1967, during his escape into hippiedom, his brief rebellion against his affluent upbringing, and he'd buried that dissolute and decadent life in the necropolis of his youthful soul, exchanging his waywardness for a career in the stock market, which, over the years, made a Solomonic treasure for him and those who'd invested, with his dice rolls, in Wall Street's floating craps game.

Now, the floor was a tangerine-and-indigo chessboard; he was standing in the rank and file of its tiles. When he turned on the shower, the water gushed aquamarine. The green freshet and brown soap mixed with his purple flesh, creating an ambiguous miscellany of hues, the LeRoy Neiman pallet of an Amazonian macaw.

There was no way he could contemplate going to work. After all, who would believe he was his old self, that he hadn't flipped out, with one foot in the butterfly farm? Thank God he lived by himself, and thank the good Lord that he was his own boss, could take a long-overdue vacation if he so chose. But he had omnipotent clients to confer with, in person, who would take extreme umbrage if he attempted to strategize with them over the horn.

Perhaps if he got back in bed, slept all day and night, tried the whole 5:40 routine over, the next morning, everything would revert to its pedestrian complexion.

He phoned his trusted secretary of thirty years. Lil was surprised; he'd missed only five times in her tenure (she remembered the day and year of every one). She expressed her regret that he had a "bad sniffle." He thanked her, hung up, then plunged into the sheets, as though they might act as a baptismal stream and return him to his natural flesh colors, bring his psychedelic bedroom (the entire condo?) back from the bad-acid flashback messing with his success.

Theodore Life

For perhaps a decade, maybe considerably longer (time was even more amorphous to him than was his idea of death), Theodore Life labored under a misunderstanding: he'd been afflicted with a pervasive condition that made him appear happy, from morning to night.

Friends labeled him as being "Earth's most positive person." Perfect strangers unexpectedly lauded his character, singing the highest praises for his "upbeat cheeriness." His underlings at Wong & Stein Computer USA had nothing but kudos for their motherboard-QA supervisor, adjudging him to be a "really good guy." He was "everybody's best friend," "salt-of-the-earth Theo," "Life-of-the-party Teddy Life," the "go-the-extra-mile Ted" you'd give your life to be like.

In point of fact, he abhorred being thought of this way, especially since he knew, deep down, that he abominated people — all of humanity — hated himself even more rancorously, loathed the prospect of not knowing how to reverse things, reconcile, or bring to closure, his overwhelming discontent.

One day, he bought in to his first happy thought. He bludgeoned his boss, in the executive washroom, then went postal, in the sterile, frigid assembly unit, shooting dead forty-three fellow employees, with five semiautomatic pistols he'd bought at a gun show, finally turning two of them on himself.

When Wong & Stein's security squad arrived, Theodore Life was slumped over his excessively tidy desk, his face frozen in a genuine smile.

The Afternoon of the Killer Iguana

OK. So I spent that entire morning (my fourth in a row, to be truthful) staying in the condo, banging out a new manuscript. (I guess I should confess I'm a wordsmith, a hard-boiled-crime-fiction writer, with eight to twelve paperbacks published each year.) And it was plenty sunny, to boot. I admit it — I'm a workaholic, a glutton for my kind of rewarding punishment. We all know that not-so-old motto (minted by . . . was it Barbarella? Jane Fonda?) "No pain, no gain."

So to give my dray-horse self a sugar cube (a Pavlovian reward for good behavior), I drove over to Sea's Edge, the resort next door, where I've been a member in infrequent good standing (I only go on retreat, to Fort Lauderdale, three times a year), hoping to locate a lounge chair under the shade of clustered poolside palm trees, peruse the Sunday *New York Times*, check out the bikinied "cheese," "chone," and then "cop a few z's" (as we used to say in the pre-Vietnam sixties), before heading back, for a routine steam bath (my condo boasts a deluxe Finnish sauna), shower, decision-time about the night's restaurant.

OK. So the sugar cube tasted good. Soon, I was into the swinging thick of things, completely absorbed by the *Times'* incisive articles, when, of a sudden, I sensed people surrounding me — guests brandishing cell phones and cameras, positioning themselves to snap prime shots.

I surfaced from riots in Putin's St. Petersburg, Ahmadinejad's visit to Saudi Arabia, tornadoes ravaging Alabama, religious freedom in China, to find a menacing four-foot-long lizard (I had to be told the chameleon was an iguana, later, by a nearby sunbather, who'd visited Costa Rica), standing on point, beside my deck chair, not eight inches from my vulnerable body.

On seeing this prehistoric behemoth, my heart froze. I was certain curtains were within striking distance. The thing was so damn close to me, I could almost feel its claws, its spiny dorsal scales, touch its deep-green, rough skin, and snap off its preposterously elongated, black-striped tail. It was much too up-close-and-personal for comfort. (I recall remarking, to my terrified mind, that it seemed to have a wattle under its chin, like those of wild turkeys I see in my yard, at home.)

OK. So I didn't dare move. I, too, assumed point. Suddenly, I was able to sympathize with celebrities stalked by the paparazzi (I write under pseudonyms). I envisioned my fleshy, way-past-middle-age body appearing on a zillion zillion YouTube downloads, my story in the following week's *National Enquirer*, *Star*: "Man-Eating Feral Everglades Iguana Consumes 'Mack Fungal, P.I.' Creator At Ritzy Resort In Fort Lauderdale."

Then, just as abruptly, the iguana bypassed me, climbed a nearby palm tree, and disappeared into the swaying, primordial fronds. I rose from my urine-sullied, towel-covered cushion, gathered up my detritus, and hightailed it (no pun intended, I assure you), back to my condo.

Pretty much so, that horrific near-death experience shattered the climax of Mack Fungal's latest caper. Face it. Could you concentrate on anything, once a giant iguana came within inches of your throat, nose, gonads? Well, I, for one, decidedly could not.

And that was the end of my getaway, three days early. Florida was public enemy number one, in my book.

As for my new book (it came out two years late), I changed its title from *Murder at Sea's Edge* to *The Afternoon of the Killer Iguana*.

Planet of the Ever-Aging Freaks

Everywhere, in every direction, from the main observation post in our sealed-off sphere, I can see, through a heavily tinted nexus-scope, a crater-pocked, suppurating lunar landscape populated with deformed creatures, each of them considerably beyond an estimable age, maneuvering like amebas, crashing like atoms, bouncing off each other, eighty-eight hours a day, darkness never arriving (a very eerie world, this, located somewhere between the Never belt and the farthest star in the Nowhere galaxy) . . . creatures who, despite knowing each other, on sight, sound, scent, touch, taste, become strangers, on first bite, dense-genital penetration, only regaining intimacy when pulling apart, then resuming their business of existing, in plain sight of the perpetually ignited sky.

These poikilothermal masses of nature's freak realm are so old, they're incapable of procreation, and yet they do endure, somehow keeping the planet's weird equilibrium from conforming with the laws of entropy. Otherwise, this world would wobble out of orbit, set us mortals, who survive in our biosphere, adrift, maroon us in an oblivion of endless darkness.

May these poor monsters continue beyond infinity!

A Perfect Fit

By the relatively ripe young age of fifty-five, Harry Barfiddle Cox IV had been married, if not divorced, twenty-six times.

He craved the initial intricacies of conjugality but disdained its day-to-day complications, which would set in sooner than later, in most cases. Naturally, he expected each of his spouses to embrace the fact that he had a troika of working penises, learn to service, simultaneously, his three phalli.

In the beginning of each new relationship, his trinal unit proved to be amusing, to say the least, a stimulating challenge for his better halves and for him. He'd show patience, at the inception of every marriage, while his new wife got used to his ins and outs, bent over backwards, literally, to satisfy him and herself. Some of his mates actually got the hang of things, for a while, anyway, until the predictable symptoms would set in — urethral chafing (from his pencil-sized uppermost appendage), bleeding anal lesions (from his low-lying probe), not to mention good old-fashioned vaginal soreness — causing each spouse to cry "Uncle," "*Basta*," eventually, call it quits, seek annulment, divorce, or just pack up and limp away, leaving no forwarding address.

In truth, at fifty-five, Harry Barfiddle Cox IV desperately and deeply desired a lasting relationship, not another marriage of inconvenience.

To this end, he elected to have a double penectomy. He'd keep the most prodigious of his three sex organs; after all, he still had his pride.

But when he awakened, in Almighty Redeemer Hospital, he found that his surviving member was not "Mr. Anal" but his peashooter, "Mr. Urethra."

While in the step-down ward, Harry Barfiddle Cox IV met Virginia Faith Chatter, who was recovering from a botched hysterectomy — a permanently sutured vagina and rectum.

"At least they left me with a pee-hole that works," she said.

Harry knew, in that instant, that he'd met his wife for life.

Thief Ants

Six weeks ago, you experienced a reasonably pleasant and restful retreat — a getaway to Honolulu.

To be sure, the only thing to mar your vacation was a seemingly innocuous infestation of thief ants, tiny creatures visible, if barely, to your naked eye, battalions, brigades, and divisions of the bellicose insects, invading the twin sinks, stove- and countertops, coffee maker and toaster, skittering in maddening fashion — an army, despite its soldiers' sixteenth-of-an-inch size, threatening your physical and emotional balance, a colossal juggernaut expropriating the time-share condo.

Soon, you became an expert in taking out those scurrying lives, smashing one at a time, with a paper napkin, squashing them in their tracks — sometimes ten per napkin.

When you'd leave the spacious apartment, to sunbathe or dine along Waikiki Boulevard, you'd envision the commandos regrouping, calling up new troops, from somewhere deep in the building's plumbing labyrinth or through elaborate trenches and catacombs in the cabinetry below the kitchen's array of appliances.

When your seven-day stay concluded, you were reluctant to leave. You'd grown addicted to your role as resident exterminator. There was no denying the rush of accomplishment you got from systematically extirpating hundreds . . . hundreds . . . *thousands* of formic factotums.

And that sensation persisted well into your first week home. During lulls at work, you'd go to the coffee lounge, scour the countertops, for signs of pismiric infestation; ditto in your cramped apartment's kitchen. But your reconnaissance was to no avail.

Withdrawal finally ran its course, and you forgot about the Honolulu killing fields.

That was a month ago. A few days later, your dreams began being assailed by strange premonitions. Your sleep was plagued with excessive restiveness. Nestled among your sheets, you kept scratching yourself. Your flesh and its thick hair twitched uncontrollably. Even your anus beckoned your fingers, with disconcerting frequency, demanding they ream it. Worse, the selfsame irritation flared during waking.

The creeping, crawling feeling finally overran your mouth, nostrils, eyelids, and ears, demanding you poke, rub, and spelunk them constantly.

Only then did you grow sufficiently concerned to drive to a nearby emergency room, where the entire team of physicians was utterly befuddled.

Now, you're being ambulanced back home. Within hours, Yancy's Pest Control will be at your door, prepared to seal you in, perform the fumigation.

Apt. 19 M
Beau

One almost normal morning, on the twenty-fourth day of the eighth month, in the fifth year of the twenty-first century, Isadore Wickersham "Beau" Beauregard left his nineteenth-floor apartment, pulled the door shut, and headed west, fifty-eight paces, toward the elevator. Little did he realize that a hurricane of pure boredom was bearing down on him, from out of nowhere, and that he and it were on a collision course.

When car two reached the subterranean third level, he exited, suffering a slight episode of dizziness, which he attributed to the elevator's inordinately swift descent. He entered the long corridor, made a ninety-degree turn, covered the same fifty-eight paces he'd taken on nineteen, this time heading due east, toward the far end of the hall.

There, he pressed the button to summon the garage elevator. A much smaller car, more like a cage, arrived and carried him two floors deeper into the earth.

He exited, this time right, walking five steps east, through a metal door with a porthole window, then fourteen more steps, to his '85 Plymouth Reliant. But something kept him from opening the door, doing his seating-and-key routine of twenty years; indeed, he was overcome with full-blown boredom.

Immediately, he turned, reversed his journey — fourteen steps to the metal door with the porthole window, five to the two-flight-trip garage elevator, fifty-eight paces, due west, to the main elevator bank, in the far end of the subterranean third level, the fifteen-floor ascent to the nineteenth story, fifty-eight paces, due east, to his apartment. He opened the door, but before he could pull it shut, boredom forced its way in with him.

For the rest of the morning, all afternoon, into the night, Beau retraced his paces from apartment to Reliant, Reliant to apartment, in an effort to elude boredom. By midnight, only *he* was exhausted. They'd made the circuit God knows how many times (he'd quit counting at two hundred ninety-two).

But even when he threw himself into bed, fully dressed, he knew boredom would be there in the morning and that neither of them would ever leave the building again.

Breaking Out

Then, one seemingly status quo Tuesday a.m., just like that, he made a snap decision to leave his house, buck, stark, jaybird, as-the-day-he-was-born naked, undressed, to the nines, from head to head to toe, not to make a fashion statement but to exhibit himself as a clothing-optionalist.

Quite simply, unambiguously, unqualifiedly, he was totally fed up with feeling fettered, constrained. Over thirty-five years of strict rigidity, conforming to codes of conduct and custom, he'd developed a silent but festering penchant for anomie, which, when it finally gestated, broke out of his raiment, like a three-foot Guinea worm, manifesting itself as an uncontainable desire to go au naturel, in the birthday-suit raw, in public.

That morning, he left his house, headed for the bus stop, boarded, stepped off, three blocks from his job, wearing not a stitch, save for his brown lunch bag, dangling from his right hand, flopping, in time, with his wagging penis.

That his appearance had raised no brows, not any, so far as he had observed, came as no surprise, really. After all, he was, in every respect he could reckon, precisely the same person he'd always been, with the one slight exception that he had absolutely nothing to hide from himself.

This feeling of complete openness was reassuring. Being nude reminded him of his fundamental humanity, allowed him to appreciate his sense of individuality, in a whole new light, gave him renewed confidence that he could do anything anyone might ask of him.

Arriving home, he got dressed, ate, climbed into bed.

Wednesday, he left nakeder. He'd shaved his pubic hair.

Making the Grand Tour

Now that you've returned to the land of nonstop baseball, college and pro football, NASCAR, tourney bowling, you feel right at home, again. No more big ideas about "broadening your cultural landscape" by trudging behind a motor-mouth tour guide, from museum to church, river to statue to tower and arch.

And thank God for your good old triple-hard bed, instead of that foundered rackabones of a lumpy mattress in that Left Bank fleabag-pigsty-dump of a hotel hidden away in some cat-howling back alley, within spitting distance of the Deluxemburger Gardens, a hotel capable of housing a flea circus, not a bunch of St. Louis roughs and their missuses, off on their once-in-a-life grand tour of Gay (for sure) Paree.

And thank God for homegrown Bud and brats; them gooey French vittles ain't anything to write home about.

And as for their naked-girlie follies, they've got nothing on Sauget's finest lap-dance ladies.

Best of all is that those two too-close-to-the-bone patdowns they did on you, in Charles de Gallbladder and O'Hair, are now all behind you — that's squirrely stuff!

No matter how much you hated your trip to Paris, you don't give the stiffs on the line the slightest satisfaction. When they bad-mouth the frogs, offer you their "freedom fries," call you an unpatriotic bastard, a traitor, for siding with the frog-fags, who didn't join our boys in *Iraq*, you scoff at their lack of class, call them assholes.

Deep down, you wish you'd never listened to the missus, had stuck to your guns, knowing the frogs *are* fags, insisted that you take your usual summer vacation, to Branson.

The Light of Day

After half a century of scribbling verse, either meditatively, in one place, for hours, or on the run, with frenzied ecstasy, resorting to every convenient form of material upon which to record his volcanic creativity — notebooks, toilet-paper scrolls, parking tickets, backs of canned-food labels and personal checks, roadside-restaurant paper napkins, special-order calf-, lamb-, and kidskin folios — he needed to find some more-durable means of preserving his immemorial thoughts.

He feared computers' corruption and obsolescence. In point of fact, he'd actually posted all his poems on a website specially crafted to his needs, and within a few months, it had been hacked, all his precious entities maliciously rewritten a dozen times each, at least, leaving him with ten thousand unidentifiable palimpsests.

It went without saying (if not literally) that it would take all his intestinal fortitude and ingenuity to prevent another wholesale desecration, cataclysmic extirpation, of his life's work, to which end he set about profoundly cogitating, until an efficacious solution presented itself.

Within days, he'd embarked on a novel course of action, by which he'd be able to conserve each new poem. He began kneading his feces into handy tablets, upon which, at a certain stage in the drying process, he'd use a $6\frac{1}{4}$-inch screwdriver to carve each stroke of each letter of each poetic word, until a complete poem was solidified, which he'd file away, in a coded clamshell case, and place on a shelf in his basement's private library, each tile impervious to mildew, mold, silverfish, foxing.

Soon, he grew adept with his timing, making his bowel movements coincide with his brainstorms.

But to his mortal dread, for six weeks before his demise, he suffered exceedingly agonizing constipation — it wasn't so much the physical pain as it was the frustration of being *completely* stoppled.

Simply stated, his last forty-two poems never saw the light of day.

New Carpeting

It all began, as far as you could recall, when some higher-up in the company where you worked instructed some other higher-up, just slightly lower on the corporate totem pole, to have new carpet installed in the hall immediately outside the Strategy Room, containing your cubicle — yours, along with those of thirty-two other facilitators (a fancy euphemism for "order fillers," who, with a few keystrokes, move product from fabrication to finishing to storage to distribution, ensuring the pickers, packers, tapers, strappers, and shippers get merchandise out the door, with expeditious expertise . . . that merchandise, exclusively toilet seats).

It all began early one Monday, when the Calabrese Bros. Carpet crew ripped up the worn covering and crumbling padding, scraped the hallway's floor, hammered in tack-strips, smoothed on the glue, stretched the new carpet and tamped it down along the edges — a loud nuisance that distracted you, all morning and afternoon.

If the clamor and din and general chaos were disconcerting, the vapors infiltrating the space where you functioned were worse; they were asphyxiating. You and your associates in the Strategy Room came down with watery eyes, headaches, light-headedness.

One not-so-aggravating side effect was that you went home, that day, with a buzz, a rush that left you hallucinating slightly and with an overall feeling of mild elation — something you'd not felt in twenty-five years.

The fumes took almost a week to fully dissipate. During that time, your yield increased five-fold. The higher-up in charge of the Strategy Room took notice. The following Monday, he summoned you to his double cubicle.

"To what do you attribute your sudden upsurge in output?"

You hadn't a clue, lest it had something to do with the glue. You were the thirty-third facilitator to be interviewed, the thirty-third to give precisely the same response.

Seven days later, Calabrese Bros. came in and began tearing out the "old" carpet, installing new.

After that, the hall got fresh carpeting weekly.

White Asparagus

Lately, sleep and he haven't made good bedfellows. Indeed, it's been MII — missing in inaction. That necessary component to his good constitution (mental, physical, spiritual) has been leaving him for pallorous dead. And as his nightless nights have turned into weeks, a decided transformation has grown robust: he's become a white asparagus.

His fellow workers shun him. His four remaining cats hiss at him; they refuse to lie in his bed, let him fondle them. The neighbor widow no longer strays into his yard, with Linzer tortes, Saturday and Sunday a.m.'s. The mailman's quit kibitzing with him. His doctor, last visit, donned a surgical mask, as if his patient were contagious. Only the local greengrocer recognizes him.

He's down to two and a half ounces. His urine smells exceedingly sulfuric. He feels as if he's been buried alive.

It's not probable, is it, he ponders, *that all this could have something to do with guilt, guilt over euthanizing Rocky, my prize Sphynx?* But what choice had he but to do the humane thing? After all, Rocky's seizures had recurred even after upping the insulin. The vet had been stymied.

This evening, he's going to take a prolonged steam, down at Mustafa's Health Baths, in hopes of blanching the whiteness from his spear, putting his vegetable self behind him, getting back to his sleep-regulated humanity, where everyone (save the greengrocer) will recognize him, including his four cats — Sugar Ray, Ali, Joe Louis, Roberto Durán — who'll forgive him, for KO'ing Rocky.

Apt. 12 R–T
Java Man

This Saturday morning, as every a.m., too early for the world, you drive the few hundred feet from your high-rise to the nonjudgmental corner Starbucks. You're in a tizzy (you might say desperate, rabid) to get your caffeine fix. Without it — that artificial pick-me-upper — you're not worth an even-less-than-lackluster shit. Deprived, you'd be dead meat, burnt toast, history.

As it is, you're a walking, breathing success story, a poster child for the efficacy of corporate greed, a guinea pig for insidious chemical modification. Call it like it is: a tantalizing form of water torture.

Over the short long haul, you've been programmed to sacrifice everything, for it. And to what end? Fourteen venti decafs a week? *Decaf*, mind you! It would hardly seem plausible. It's supposed to be Starbucks's most innocuous product, not the toxic bunker-buster it is — their good-to-the-last-drop baby-boomer answer to mom, apple pie, and God.

That you're hooked, you'd be the first to confess. (Though you wish it weren't so, you know Hazelden is out of the question.)

And now that you're cogitating about it, you're positive Starbucks has hatched a conspiracy to awaken the drowsing Java man in each of us.

Sitting on Top of the World

OK, so where did everyone go, this Monday morning? There ain't a soul in the joint. Not even a mouse is stirring, in this empty restaurant, no one but me and the trans fats sizzling on the grill, watched over by short-order maestro Bobby, flipping and nudging mounds of hash browns, with his spatula.

I mean, this is a real eerie scene. Here, you got three waitresses twiddling their thumbs, as if they were (the thumbs) divining rods searching for customers.

So this is what they mean, on TV, when they say "recession." Dead! Everything's deader than the proverbial dormouse. To be the only paying regular (or irregular, for that matter) is a sight I've never seen, here at Tenderhook's Café.

At this rate, the joint'll be out of business, in a month, and I'll have to drive three miles out of my way, if I intend to grab grub on my way to work, which I can't say I'm too damn keen on doing.

Then again, things keep up this way, maybe it won't matter, since I could be out of a job, myself. After all, when the gas gets to nine or twelve bucks a gallon, nobody's gonna be buying the cars I make, anyway . . . unless our assembly line, out at Fenton, can be converted into making Johnny On The Spots — "automatic comfort stations" — for all of us foreclosure junkies to live in, like FEMA trailers, as we watch America go down the crapper, with us sitting on top of the world, you might say.

Either way, it's goddamn empty in Tenderhook's, today. I hate to see Flora, Billie Jean, and Aretha twiddling their divining rods, searching even for mice.

The Education of X2Q

When X2Q exited Techno-Acres pod-module APZ, having determined it was time to slip outside, disburden the tanks of his abdominal sewage units, he noticed that Electropolis's HAZMAT lawn hygienists had neglected vacuuming the surrounding zoysia — those areas restricted to residents' discharges.

He was appalled to witness the fecal/urinous eyesores, which, in the three weeks since he'd last jettisoned, had swollen into fly-infested berms and drumlins.

"Goddamn those municipal workers!" he beeped. "The bastards always seem to go out on strike whenever it suits 'em, just to keep even with inflation! They don't give a rat's turd about the other guy — selfish bastards!"

Fortunately, X2Q, just in the nick of time, found an unsullied air-conditioner-condenser cove, only used by cats, squirrels, coyotes, badgers, weasels (dogs knew better than to frequent that preserve), where he could evacuate his unabsorbed intake, and in relative privacy, to boot. (Always, he'd be "going" amidst dozens of other occupants doing *their* duties, taking *their* obligatory constitutionals, in plain sight of their neighbors; indeed, not since he was in the Mechanical Coalescence Lab, undergoing complete R and R — retrofitting and rehab — to extend his existence by five hundred chrono-parsecs, had he known such untrammeled refuge from public scrutiny.) But no sooner had he opened his titanium plumbing's petcock, relaxed the hydraulics of his molybdenum sphincter, than he was set upon by a squadron of HAZMAT hygienists maneuvering a six-foot-diameter articulated suction tube connected to an antiquated mobile rocket launcher.

Sputtering, flashing, terrified, for his operational allotment, X2Q hunkered down, squatting on his struts, sullying himself, anticipating the worst, which, in a whoosh, happened. He was sucked up, in the compaction contraption.

For a month, he tunneled under metric tons of landfill, his gears, cogs, and circuitry gummed up and clogged, until a semblance of solar radiation summoned him and he emerged infinitely wiser, illuminated, his ocular receptors suddenly open to the ways of the world, for his having survived the horrible ordeal at Techno-Acres.

Having found enlightenment, truth, salvation, lubrication, X2Q, from that visionary day forth, emptied his effluents indoors, into APZ's nuclear cooling pool.

Ignatius

Each evening, for at least a decade, now, you've safely sailed the Sleep Ocean, in the chambered shell of a sea-monster nautilus.

You can't remember when or under what circumstances the cephalopod mollusk and you first met or how you reached such amicable commensalism (in exchange for Ignatius's protection, you intravenously feed him the nutrients of your dreams, through your powers of suggestion).

To this day, the relationship flourishes. You've visited every port on the ocean's vast shores. Ignatius has participated in the filtration of your anxieties, bottom-fed on the detritus of your life, learned more about you than you know about yourself. You've mastered thousands of tongues, cultures. In truth, you prefer this existence to that of your daytime. It's infinitely more interesting, compelling, rewarding.

For the last six months, Ignatius and you have been concocting a plan to avoid having to leave each other every sunrise, devise a way for your symbiosis to extend around the clock.

Recently, you've been arriving at daylight later and later. Excuses for your tardiness at work have grown flimsy. You've already been issued sixty-five demerits; the sixty-sixth will result in your termination.

Tomorrow, you won't awaken, safe inside the chambers of your Ignatian dream-life.

Monday, but Worse

Tenderhook's isn't doing a whole hell of a lot better, this rainy Tuesday a.m., either, after yesterday morning's breakfast for one — me.

Right now (it's 7:15, and I've been here since 6:30), the joint's hosting exactly a ratio of one to one — three customers for three thumb-twiddling waitresses, or, I should say, waitresses in waiting, waiting not to have babies (though I bet if they could each have sextuplet customers, they'd do it in a St. Louis minute . . . which, come to think of it, ain't all that frigging quick) but waiting to get their taxi tip-meters tripped. After all, these gals gotta eat, too, put food on their tables at home, just like here.

But nothing's smokin' but Bobby's hash browns, on the grill, and they must be wondering (the hash browns) when they'll be doled out, "plated," along with the sausages, ham steaks, gravy and biscuits, eggs every which way but raw (more than once, I've sighted the beginnings of baby chicks in my extra-runny sunny-side-ups, though) — the basics of breakfast-as-usual, for us hungry blue necks.

Only, on top of all this rip-roaring silence, every window facing the extra-loud rain-wet highway, letting in every goddamn tire whine from eighteen wheelers, gear shifting and muffler rumble and roar and snort from dump trucks, buses, Winnebagos, and ambulances, along with the regular road-rage junkers of guys like me, heading to assembly lines, warehouses, ditches, and to luxury subdivisions, for dry-walling, electric, plumbing . . . every frigging window is as wide open as it can go, in a dumber than stupid attempt, by the absentee manager (who doesn't even come in till 8:00), to cool Tenderhook's down to semi-tropical-desert, trying to get nature (in this case, the greenhouse-gassed rush-hour outside air) to do the job of this joint's busted rooftop air-conditioners. I'm sweating like a stuck monkey, already, from the heat fleeing Bobby's unplated hash browns, no matter they're all the way back in the kitchen.

Suddenly, something's moving, out of my left eye's far side. At first, I think it's my floaters, acting up as normal; then it's not them but a couple or three of those pain-in-the-ass regulars, with gray furry coats and unshaven whiskers, that crawl out of Tenderhook's woodwork whenever no one's looking or whenever J.C., the buser/janitor, calls in drunk.

Jesus, just what Aretha, Flora, and Billie Jean need — a herd of bottom feeders who come in, eat and run, but cheese out, when it comes to the tips.

Kicking the Bucket

He had not the foggiest of an inkling as to how he got both feet stuck in the bucket, the wooden one he used to collect his cow's milk, which he'd release from her bulbous udder, dawn and dusk, by orgasmically sucking on her luscious, throbbing teats.

But there he was, nonetheless, rolling on the ground, drenched in hot milk, unable to stand up, with his milkmaid leaning over him, hangdog, doubtless frustrated by the cessation of his manipulations, steadfastly lowing, licking him, from seed cap to booted toe.

And there he lay, all afternoon and evening, fatigued from trying to extricate his feet from the bucket.

After seventy-odd hours, the matriarch of his modest Guernsey herd began bellowing, from the pain of not being milked.

Owing to the vast pastoral spaces between farms, nobody came to their rescue, for two weeks. And when his nearest neighbors, twenty-five miles away, finally did arrive, there was nothing left to save, save a sun-scorched cadaver and a carcass lying side by side, in black-putrefactive rigor mortis, possessing, on their creamy, decaying faces, expressions of unconsummated lust, unrequited love — woeful barnyard Romeo and his star-crossed, ever-submissive heifer, Juliet.

Apt. 21 Q
Willkommen

Perhaps eight or nine months ago, Mr. Sarkozy took decided note of the shiny-new cobalt-blue Porsche 911 Carrera 4S parked two slots over from his allocated space in the large garage serving his high-rise.

Mr. Sarkozy generally had no interest whatsoever in things automotive. Indeed, over the previous thirty years, he'd lost his ability to distinguish one make from another. All that mattered was that his car got him to and from work, which was justification enough for him to keep from trading in his trusty '82 Ford, a black LTD Country Squire station wagon, with simulated wood paneling and wide whitewalls. He pampered his vehicle, and it pampered him.

But how could he help admiring such an exquisite jewel? That 911 was a thing of rare beauty, an art object first and a machine only by functional default. Every morning, when he walked to his LTD Country Squire, he made a point of weaving past that immaculate Porsche. That was when it all began.

Possibly a month or just three weeks later, a second brand-new 2005 Porsche 911 Carrera 4S, with the same cobalt-blue finish, blue cabriolet top, and glistening five-spoke alloy wheels, appeared in the garage. Its owner also must have admired the original Porsche, coveted it enough to purchase one for himself. Mr. Sarkozy found this copycatting astonishing, at best.

Just days later, returning home after work, he saw two more Porsches, clones of the other pair. This he found difficult to assimilate. Not knowing how to react, he began trembling, sweating, laughing nervously. The night watchman, staring into the security monitors, remarked Mr. Sarkozy's extremely strange behavior.

Three months after the first Porsche's manifestation, half of the garage slots were filled with cobalt-blue '05 Porsche

911 Carrera 4S Cabriolets. The place resembled the lot of Reich Motors, Ltd., which he passed on his route to work and back.

A fortnight ago, Mr. Sarkozy noticed that all the spaces in the garage, a total of fifty-eight, were filled with the same Porsche 911 Carrera 4S . . . all the spaces but one, that was — his.

Yesterday, exiting the underground garage, Mr. Sarkozy was inundated by a latent sensation. He felt anxious, disenfranchised, lonely; his black '82 Ford LTD Country Squire wagon seemed marginalized.

By noon, he couldn't hold his concentration, stay focused on the risk profiles he was actuarializing. His sector chief inquired as to his well-being. By three o'clock, Mr. Sarkozy, mentally spent, requested early leave, which was granted.

Driving home, he U-turned into Reich Motors, Ltd. three sales associates vectored in on him. That evening, he returned, to his high-rise, in a shiny-new black Porsche 911 Carrera 4S Cabriolet.

Grudgingly, the cobalt-blue garage welcomed him.

Just in Case

Although you know no one, no one in the world, you've become a Verizon Wireless cell-phone subscriber, just in case . . . not just in case somebody might call, some stranger trying to locate someone whose number approximates your own, or just in case you're mortally wounded and urgently need 911 or require a tow truck to pull you out of a ravine, but just in case you want to call yourself, to see whether, possibly, you're there, if you find yourself, at times, out of touch. After all, it's quite reassuring to know that if you call, you'll most likely answer.

More important, the sales rep at the Verizon mall kiosk told you that if you do get lost and have your lawyer obtain a court order for a search warrant (forget "probable cause"), you can have Verizon locate your whereabouts, even if your cell phone isn't in use, just turned on, track you within three hundred yards of yourself.

What a godsend this exquisite technology is, another cog in a global-positioning system, right there on your belt or in your shirt pocket. Now, you can follow yourself into your most personal spaces — your home, the john, the confessional, the liquor store.

And if you ever need to check where you've been, Verizon assures you access to their records, which they'll keep for a few years . . . maybe forever.

The Secret Life of an Attaché Case

He and his oxblood Vaqueta-leather attaché case were joined at the hip, inextricable. And as with Mary's little nursery-rhyme lamb, wherever he went, his attaché was sure to go.

It had been that way for many decades. He and his attaché were an item, the topic of conversation, not so much at work (because for all his male colleagues on floors three through sixteen, attachés were de rigueur) but whenever he took a female companion to dinner (fancy restaurant or franchise drive-thru), attended a baseball or football game, rock concert or political rally, at the local stadium, or went jogging, worshiped at church, shopped at the mall.

Indeed, his attaché was a sort of courtesan, since it slept beside his nightstand, as if, at any moment, it might leap into bed with him. In fact, over the years, he and his attaché had developed a blood tie or the closest thing to it: love.

Whenever people saw him coming, they couldn't help but wonder what was in his attaché. Highly classified Pentagon documents? Purloined diagrams of the latest weapons systems being developed at Los Alamos or Livermore? Kinky transgender underwear? Erotically stimulating devices? Exotic designer drugs? A "dirty bomb"? Botulinum toxins? Sarin gas? Airborne HIV spores? Cigar boxes filled with tarantulas? A spitting cobra, ready to rise to his flute's beckoning?

Admittedly, people didn't know what to make of his egregiously unorthodox behavior — accompanying his attaché wherever it went. At times, it appeared that it, not he, had the upper hand, was the alpha male of that pack of two.

He never did open his attaché, not even at work, which lent mystique to his already enigmatic idiosyncrasy.

When he died, his single-sentence will directed that he be cremated, his ashes placed in his attaché, and that they be buried — inextricable, as in life.

Horseman, Pass By

It had taken him nearly three years to grow used to the suburban-St. Louis Starbucks that appropriated the family-owned corner drugstore in his pre-WWII slate-roofed-Tudor neighborhood, accept its intrusion on the urban serenity . . . three years to realize that the people had spoken by voting corporate America into the previously secluded, tree-lined streets, given it the keys to the city, without even being lobbied; they'd expressed their democratic *yea* for progress . . . three years to fully appreciate that its blight was benign, its impact on traffic patterns innocuous, that the insidious hawker of addictive libations did little to threaten his quiet purlieus, in fact contributed to public beautification, with its taxes . . . three years to fall prey to spending his weekend a.m.'s passing time at its welcoming tables, imbibing one, two, three frappucinos while reading the *Times*, stimulating his brain with vision-inducing caffeine, being won over by the laissez-faire attitude of the place.

It took him every ounce of the nearly three years to finally surrender his antipathy toward the alien invaders taking over the world, operating out of the titanium-and-glass Death Star that had landed in Seattle's downtown industrial district.

Then, just when he saw his once dread enemy completely blend into the community, the city fathers, in their inexplicably definitive sagacity, tore out the three exquisite pear trees that crowned the boulevard immediately across from Starbucks, sank a foundation, and laid in place a black-marble base the size of a Mini Cooper, atop which they plopped a twelve-foot-tall bronze Botero — a hideous, grotesque, flabby horse and rider.

Citizens guffawed at and cursed the perverse statue. Distracted drivers crashed into each other, at the intersection. Birds, confused over having lost their leafy haunts, strafed the black atrocity, with droppings, lending to the eyesore the design of a Grévy's zebra. And he, who'd come to love lingering in Starbucks, recoiled. Repulsion and disgust, hatred bordering on insurrection, were hardly adequate nouns for what he felt. Who was responsible for this public desecration? What Greeks bore this freakish gift? How could the neighborhood get back its pear trees?

For the next three years, he sat in his local Starbucks, on weekends, gazing out at the monstrosity, seething, hissing, praying that a trash truck or bus would level it, plotting how to World Trade Center that Botero.

One Saturday, in a late autumn of his discontent, it came to him, in a feverish epiphany. On leaving, carrying his steaming frappucino-to-go, passing in the cold shadow of that ghastly statue, he splashed the coffee on gaskins, hocks, and boots. This act satisfied his primal need to destroy the adversary.

After that, he began attending Starbucks twice daily (like going to church, to take communion) before and after work, in addition to weekends, making sure to hurl a twenty-ouncer at the public art. This ritual became tantamount to pagan sacrifice.

By the following October, he noticed something curious: the black patina on all six legs was splotchy. Some barely noticeable mystical corrosion was setting up, further spurring his worship of Starbucks. Perhaps he could have an effect, make a difference, prove that one tiny voice could speak amplitudes. Quietly inspired with hope, he continued his dousing.

The seasons leached into history. Over the next decade, he flung 7300 cups of Starbucks, and the Botero, though not to the naked eye, began to suffer structural fatigue — he could tell; he just knew. The city officials showed no concern for the "weathering"; it was "expected," "natural," "enhancing."

Eventually, one twilight in May, as he sat in Starbucks, reading about the Kentucky Derby, in the *Times*, he looked up to see horse and rider tremble, tilt, topple monolithically, come to a rumbling thud on the aghast boulevard.

Exuberant, exhilarated, ecstatic with religious fervor, he took the frappucino splasher-to-go he'd ordered and, bearing witness to the collapsed statue, thrust the cup high, then chugged it with lusty gusto, in a farewell toast, screaming, "Horseman, pass by!"

Reunion Essay Questionnaire

Shock enough, it was, when I received a bulging white parcel from the institution of higher learning that graduated me into the wide, wild world of wily reality, nigh onto forty-five years ago, that fat packet containing all manner of friendly desiderata inviting me to prime myself to return to New Haven, after almost half a century, to revel in the celebration of my manifest aging, a prospect in which I had less than zero-tolerance interest, no matter the social and intellectual enticements, the appeals to my devotion to dear old alma mater.

Stupid, naive, gullible, Adam-innocent me, I opened the plump envelope (rather than trashing it summarily), cutting it just enough slack, to give it the benefit of the down-and-out doubt, allow it to inflict its presumptive spew-spell, over me, attempt to cajole me into submitting a recent photo, filling out an "anonymous" survey, updating a bio, and composing sage answers to seven inquiries (to be Web-sited).

Having a few lapsed minutes in my otherwise idle afternoon, I reviewed the seven-too-many you've-got-to-be-kidding-me queries posed by the "Class of 1963 45th Reunion Essay Questionnaire" and gasped for panic-attack breath. The interrogatories knocked me flat out of bed, on my ass, reminded me of my blue-book-exam days at Mother Yale, transported me to those stressful four-hour autos-da-fé, when I was compelled to recycle metric tons of bullshit, answering questions even the Sphinx wouldn't think up.

For a good ten minutes, I debated whether or not to invest the emotional time, in answering those deepest of heavy-duty questions, which some quorum, *minyan*, of haughty "class officers" had had the audacity to concoct, in order to give meaning to their ultra-affluent boredom.

And so it was that I reached into my *Lux et Veritas*, my lifetime's worth of pedestrian wisdom, to give back, to Yale, something that would make her proud.

Q: "How has your life differed from what you expected in 1963?"

A: "For one thing, I've had no money and no prospects since going AWOL after killing ten water buffaloes, at My Lai. Also, I took the brown acid, at Woodstock, became a roadie for the Who, then ended up at Esalen, where I was gang-raped by Allen Ginsberg and Peter Orlovsky. For the last thirty-five years, I've been the chief latrinist at Father Rosenstein's Home for the Prodigal and Damned, in Truth or Consequences, New Mexico."

Q: "What values or beliefs have guided you throughout your life? Have they changed or remained constant over time?"

A: "I firmly believe that although humanity isn't worth a shit, all women, ugly or otherwise, endowed or otherwise, willing or otherwise, should be taken advantage of, wantonly, and that I'm just the right guy for the job. Also, I've always maintained that it's a cardinal and ordinal sin not to steal from food pantries and the homeless. Indeed, I have noticed that, over the years, my values have matured. These days, I'm even willing to pilfer from children and old ladies. As for my salacious behavior, I've not ruled out pedophilia as a viable alternative lifestyle."

Q: "As you look to your life after 65, what changes in relationships and circumstances do you expect?"

A: "Most likely, my live-in lover, who has a disgusting case of AIDS, is going to knock off, within the next three months, which is pretty fine with me — quite timely, really — since I have a litter of five other HIV-positives, to pick from. And I'm hoping that Father Rosenstein will advance me, from latrinist, to his personal altar boy, thereby allowing me to take communion directly from his cock."

Q: "What, if any, new roles do you foresee for yourself?"

A: "Kaiser, dinner, cabbage, egg, spring, and jelly. Ha-ha! Just kidding! Seriously, I'm entering clown school, Monday, where I plan to study asbestos and snow removal, research the mating habits of barnacles and giant and colossal squids, and practice the relaxation techniques of Torquemada."

Q: "What hopes or fears do you have about these changes?"

A: "I'm terribly concerned not that I might get strangled by squids but that a circus lion won't find my honk-horn routine funny. I also have genuine misgivings about becoming a kaiser roll, because Father Rosenstein might mistake me for a wafer and eat me, for communion, by mistake."

Q: "What words of advice would you give to your child, grandchild or young person?"

A: "Son, when I ask for the time, don't build me a watch. More important, if given the chance, say no to life. Furthermore, ask not what you can do for your country; ask what you can do your country out of. Seriously, if someone tries to pick you up, on the street, don't be squeamish or stand-offish. Just ask, 'Your place or mine?'"

Q: "What do you wish you were doing less of? More of?"

A: "Less masturbating. More fucking. Less dreaming. More LSD trips. Less bloody stool. More tequila. Less living in a state of suspended evaporation. More living on a psychedelic-mushroom farm, in Tecate."

Having completed the "Essay Questionnaire" and actually feeling considerably headier than I'd anticipated, I decided to attend the June reunion, after all.

I mailed the packet, chock full of my complete raison d'être, including a nude photo of Barry Manilow, back to Boola Boola, and began planning out what I'd wear to each event.

Dumb

Of a sudden, he discovered himself struck dumb. His tongue, a dead slug, was profoundly numb. It wouldn't respond to his mind's compulsion to communicate with others within his immediate sphere and not so near.

When people engaged him, anticipating a response, all he could do, out of humiliating futility, was point to his throat — sign language of a primitive sort — as though this alone would absolve him of having to explain his seeming rudeness.

After a few days of such awkwardness, he didn't care to endure further scrutiny, abuse, rather stayed hidden away, holed up, in his basement's home theater, immersed in the sharp, terse barks of John Wayne, W. C. Fields's cascades of sardonic, caustic words.

Occasionally, he'd stare at himself in the mirror. He could open his mouth but couldn't get his seized tongue to wag.

Nonetheless, he managed to manufacture noise. Within a week of humming and moaning, he'd mastered a crude vocabulary of sounds, which encouraged him to venture out of the house.

His mailman thought him hilarious; the butcher assumed he'd gone off the deep end; his disgusted ninety-three-year-old mother, a resident of New Mount Zion Sunrise Assisted Living, had her caregiver eject him from the premises.

Then, of another sudden, his tongue regained sensation, flexibility.

But to his chagrin, he had nothing left to say.

Apt. 9 G
No More

Here in my high-rise, they're dropping off like flies. Some weeks, it almost seems as if it's a daily ritual.

Just this morning, I got the news, via a dittoed communiqué, from the super's office, laid outside my door, that old Schimmelpfennig croaked, yesterday, and that he's to have a military funeral, tomorrow, at Jefferson Barracks National Cemetery — full honor-guard ceremony, the whole-nine-yards schmear of rifle-toting soldiers, flag-draped casket, prerecorded taps, etc.

Last week it was ninety-three-year-old Ditch — Agatha Schuster Ditch, the crotchety old biddy who'd lived in 6 C since the sixties.

Come to think of it, you could say the high-rise is a bee-hive of dying, a twenty-two-story boneyard for the decrepit and doomed.

Shit! Next thing you know, I'll be following the crowds, to the exits, checking out, without so much as a hoot-and-a-holler shout, my only claim to fame (and that, for just a few hours, one morning), lying outside eighty-five doors: an obituary notice, from Bess Dyker's Ditto machine, announcing, to my fellow residents-in-waiting, that I'm no more and that my apartment's available.

Biographical Note

Louis Daniel Brodsky was born in St. Louis, Missouri, in 1941, where he attended St. Louis Country Day School. After earning a B.A., magna cum laude, at Yale University in 1963, he received an M.A. in English from Washington University in 1967 and an M.A. in Creative Writing from San Francisco State University the following year.

From 1968 to 1987, while continuing to write poetry, he assisted in managing a 350-person men's-clothing factory in Farmington, Missouri, and started one of the Midwest's first factory-outlet apparel chains. From 1980 to 1991, he taught English and creative writing, part-time, at Mineral Area College, in nearby Flat River. Since 1987, he has lived in St. Louis and devoted himself to composing poems and short fictions. He has a daughter and a son.

Brodsky is the author of sixty-two volumes of poetry (five of which have been published in French by Éditions Gallimard) and twenty-three volumes of prose, including nine books of scholarship on William Faulkner and eight books of short fictions. His poems and essays have appeared in *Harper's*, *Faulkner Journal*, *Southern Review*, *Texas Quarterly*, *National Forum*, *American Scholar*, *Studies in Bibliography*, *Kansas Quarterly*, *Forum*, *Cimarron Review*, and *Literary Review*, as well as in *Ariel*, *Acumen*, *Orbis*, *New Welsh Review*, *Dalhousie Review*, and other journals. His work has also been printed in five editions of the *Anthology of Magazine Verse and Yearbook of American Poetry*.

In 2004, Brodsky's *You Can't Go Back, Exactly* won the award for best book of poetry, presented by the Center for Great Lakes Culture, at Michigan State University.

Other Poetry and Short Fictions Available from Time Being Books

Yakov Azriel

Beads for the Messiah's Bride: Poems on Leviticus
In the Shadow of a Burning Bush: Poems on Exodus
Threads from a Coat of Many Colors: Poems on Genesis

Edward Boccia

No Matter How Good the Light Is: Poems by a Painter

Louis Daniel Brodsky

The Capital Café: Poems of Redneck, U.S.A.
Catchin' the Drift o' the Draft *(short fictions)*
Combing Florida's Shores: Poems of Two Lifetimes
The Complete Poems of Louis Daniel Brodsky: Volumes One–Four
Dine-Rite: Breakfast Poems
Disappearing in Mississippi Latitudes: Volume Two of *A Mississippi Trilogy*
The Eleventh Lost Tribe: Poems of the Holocaust
Falling from Heaven: Holocaust Poems of a Jew and a Gentile *(Brodsky and Heyen)*
Forever, for Now: Poems for a Later Love
Four and Twenty Blackbirds Soaring
Gestapo Crows: Holocaust Poems
A Gleam in the Eye: Volume One of *The Seasons of Youth*
Leaky Tubs *(short fictions)*
Mississippi Vistas: Volume One of *A Mississippi Trilogy*
Mistress Mississippi: Volume Three of *A Mississippi Trilogy*
Nuts to You! *(short fictions)*
Once upon a Small-Town Time: Poems of America's Heartland
Paper-Whites for Lady Jane: Poems of a Midlife Love Affair
Peddler on the Road: Days in the Life of Willy Sypher
Pigskinizations *(short fictions)*
Rated Xmas *(short fictions)*
Shadow War: A Poetic Chronicle of September 11 and Beyond, Volumes One–Five
Showdown with a Cactus: Poems Chronicling the Prickly Struggle
    Between the Forces of Dubya-ness and Enlightenment, 2003–2006
Still Wandering in the Wilderness: Poems of the Jewish Diaspora
This Here's a Merica *(short fictions)*
The Thorough Earth
Three Early Books of Poems by Louis Daniel Brodsky, 1967–1969: *The Easy
    Philosopher*, *"A Hard Coming of It" and Other Poems*, and *The Foul Rag-
    and-Bone Shop*
Toward the Torah, Soaring: Poems of the Renascence of Faith
A Transcendental Almanac: Poems of Nature
Voice Within the Void: Poems of *Homo supinus*

866-840-4334
http://www.timebeing.com

Louis Daniel Brodsky *(continued)*
The World Waiting to Be: Poems About the Creative Process
Yellow Bricks *(short fictions)*
You Can't Go Back, Exactly

Harry James Cargas *(editor)*
Telling the Tale: A Tribute to Elie Wiesel on the Occasion of His 65th
    Birthday — Essays, Reflections, and Poems

Judith Chalmer
Out of History's Junk Jar: Poems of a Mixed Inheritance

Gerald Early
How the War in the Streets Is Won: Poems on the Quest of Love and Faith

Gary Fincke
Blood Ties: Working-Class Poems

Charles Adés Fishman
Blood to Remember: American Poets on the Holocaust *(editor)*
Chopin's Piano

CB Follett
Hold and Release

Albert Goldbarth
A Lineage of Ragpickers, Songpluckers, Elegiasts & Jewelers: Selected
    Poems of Jewish Family Life, 1973–1995

Robert Hamblin
From the Ground Up: Poems of One Southerner's Passage to Adulthood
Keeping Score: Sports Poems for Every Season

William Heyen
Erika: Poems of the Holocaust
Falling from Heaven: Holocaust Poems of a Jew and a Gentile *(Brodsky and Heyen)*
The Host: Selected Poems, 1965–1990
Pterodactyl Rose: Poems of Ecology
Ribbons: The Gulf War — A Poem

866-840-4334
http://www.timebeing.com

Ted Hirschfield
German Requiem: Poems of the War and the Atonement of a Third Reich Child

Virginia V. James Hlavsa
Waking October Leaves: Reanimations by a Small-Town Girl

Rodger Kamenetz
The Missing Jew: New and Selected Poems
Stuck: Poems Midlife

Norbert Krapf
Blue-Eyed Grass: Poems of Germany
Looking for God's Country
Somewhere in Southern Indiana: Poems of Midwestern Origins

Adrian C. Louis
Blood Thirsty Savages

Leo Luke Marcello
Nothing Grows in One Place Forever: Poems of a Sicilian American

Gardner McFall
The Pilot's Daughter
Russian Tortoise

Joseph Meredith
Hunter's Moon: Poems from Boyhood to Manhood

Ben Milder
The Good Book Also Says . . . : Numerous Humorous Poems Inspired by
    the New Testament
The Good Book Says . . . : Light Verse to Illuminate the Old Testament
Love Is Funny, Love Is Sad
What's So Funny About the Golden Years
The Zoo You Never Gnu: A Mad Menagerie of Bizarre Beasts and Birds

Charles Muñoz
Fragments of a Myth: Modern Poems on Ancient Themes